WARNING

THIS BOOK BELONGS TO...

For Evie

Published by Happy Cat Books
An imprint of Catnip Publishing Ltd.
14 Greville Street
London EC1N 8SB

First published 2008
1 3 5 7 9 10 8 6 4 2
Text copyright © 2008 by Vivian French
Illustrations copyright © 2008 by Natalie Russell

ISBN  978-1-905117-85-7

Printed in China by WKT Co. Ltd.

www.catnippublishing.co.uk

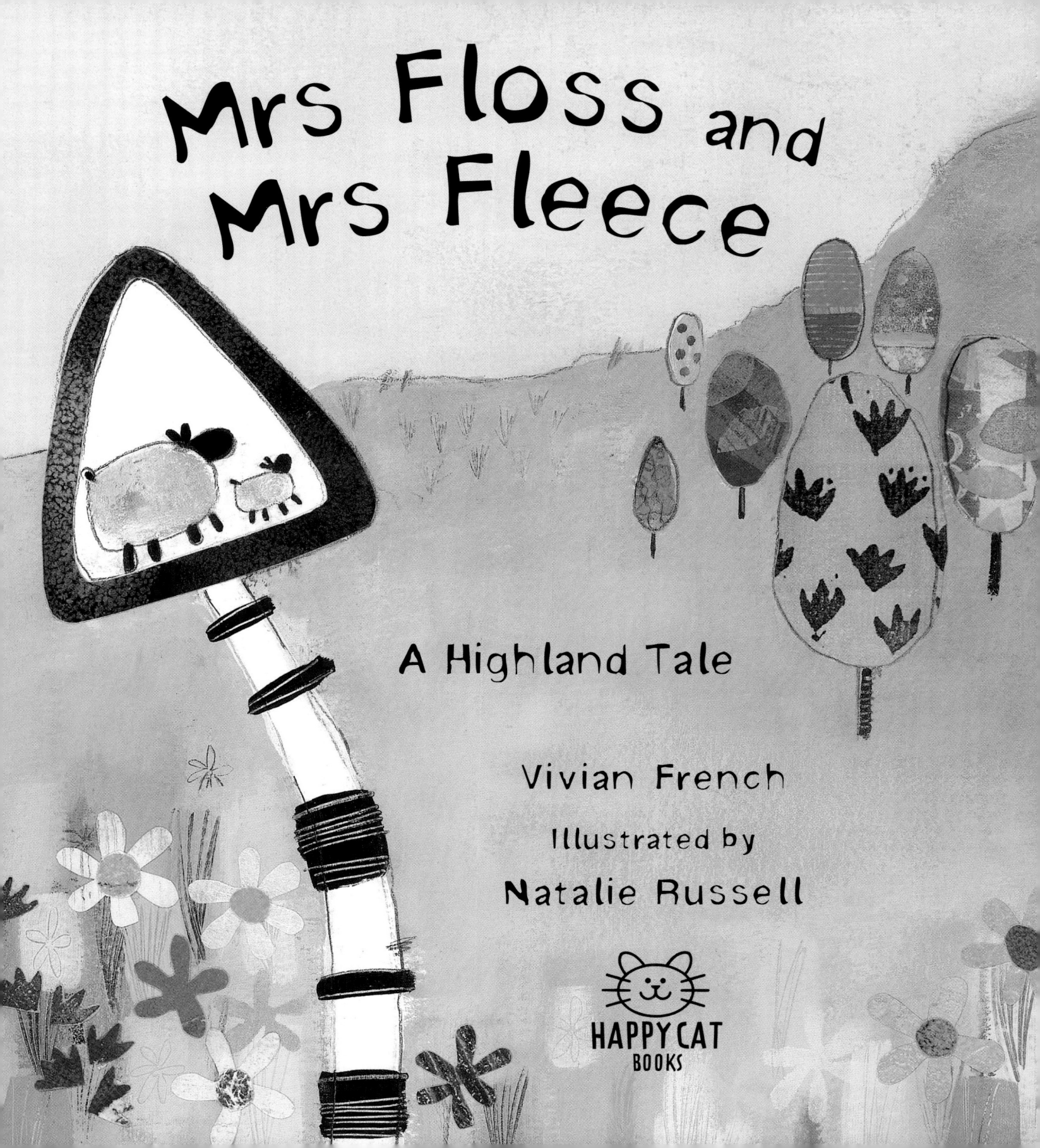

# Mrs Floss and Mrs Fleece

## A Highland Tale

Vivian French

Illustrated by

Natalie Russell

HAPPY CAT
BOOKS

Mrs Floss lived on a hill.

Mrs Fleece lived
in a valley by a
river and a road.

Mrs Floss was scared of everything.
"Oh no! Could that be the **big bad wolf?**"

Mrs Fleece was scared of nothing.

Then, one fine spring day, Mrs Floss had a lamb.

"Oooh! I'll call ye Ross!"

And so did Mrs Fleece.

"Ma ain wee Reece!"

Ross was a big bold lamb.

He soon bounced his way down the hill

looking for someone to play with.

But Reece was small and scared
and trembly, and didn't want
to play. "Awa wi ye!"
Mrs Fleece told him.

But Reece hid behind a buttercup.

"You're nae son of mine!" said Mrs Fleece, and she went to lie down in the middle of the road.

BEEP BEEP                    HONK

"**FUN!**" said Ross, and he lay down beside her.

Meanwhile, up on the hill, an anxious Mrs Floss was looking for Ross.

She looked **HERE**, and **THERE**,

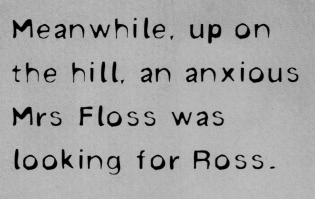

and **UP**,

SQUAWK!

she woke the BIG BAD WOLF who lived
in a cave at the very top of the hill.

RRRRRRRRrr

roared the wolf,

and he leapt and he snarled,
and he chased Mrs Floss
        down
            **down**
                **down the hill**

and across the road.

"BAAAA!"

bleated Ross, and he jumped up
and ran away as fast as he could go.

"BAAAA!" bleated Mrs Fleece, and she jumped up and ran as fast as she could go.

Reece peeped out from behind
his buttercup -
and there was Ross
and Mrs Floss
and his mother

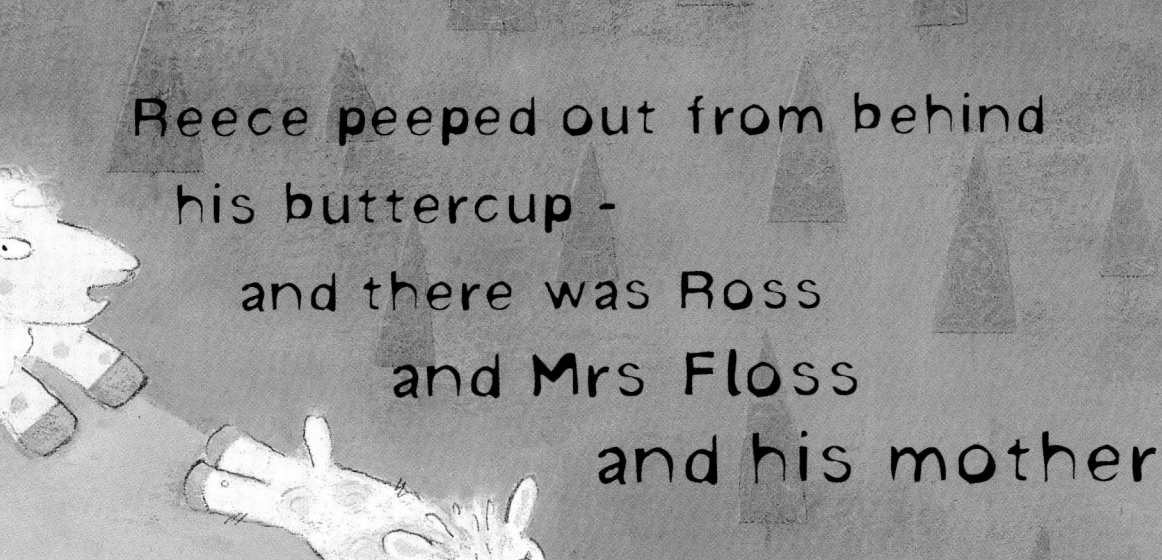

running
and running
and RUNNING
towards the river.

"MAA! MAA! WAIT FOR ME!"
called Reece.

He dashed
out, and

"YAROOOO!"
The wolf tripped over him,

and fell into the river with a

SPLASH!

"HOOORAH for Reece!"
shouted Mrs Floss and Mrs Fleece ...

but Ross said nothing at all.
He was hiding behind a daisy.